LIGHTNING STRIKE

TANYA LANDMAN

OXFORD
UNIVERSITY PRESS

Great Clarendon Street, Oxford, OX2 6DP, United Kingdom

Oxford University Press is a department of the University of Oxford.

It furthers the University's objective of excellence in research, scholarship, and education by publishing worldwide. Oxford is a registered trade mark of Oxford University Press in the UK and in certain other countries

British Library Cataloguing in Publication Data

Data available

ISBN 978-0-19-8494898

1 3 5 7 9 10 8 6 4 2

Paper used in the production of this book is a natural, recyclable product made from wood grown in sustainable forests.

The manufacturing process conforms to the environmental regulations of the country of origin.

Printed in China by Golden Cup

Acknowledgements

Cover illustration by Chaaya Prabhat

The publisher is grateful to Greta Thunberg Media for permission to use Greta Thunberg's words from her speech "Together we are unstoppable", made at the Climate Strike in New York on 21 September 2019.

The publisher would like to thank Jane Branson for writing the additional resources.

For campaigners everywhere – past, present and future –
who fight to make the world a better place.

"Together and united we are unstoppable."

GRETA THUNBERG

1

I was too angry, Mother said. I never stopped fuming. I raged about everything, every waking moment, from dawn to dusk. I even did it in my sleep, according to Mother. She said she could hear me through the floorboards. I'd lie in the makeshift bed I shared with my sisters and my brother and mumble over and over, "It ain't right. It ain't right."

But it wasn't right! None of it! Working all hours yet we'd struggle to pay the rent every single week. We never, ever had enough to eat. We were always teetering on the brink of ruin. How could anyone live the way we did, see the things we saw, hear the things we heard and not be angry? If you weren't fuming, you just weren't paying attention.

Mother said I was wasting my time fretting. But then Mother was a devoted Christian. She said everything that happened was God's will. He moved in mysterious ways and we had to accept it with good grace.

But I couldn't, no matter how hard I tried.

I had a list as long as my arm of all the things I thought were wrong with the world. No, even longer. The list was as long as both my arms. And my legs.

Right at the top of the list was Mrs Jones who lived next door. She had phossy jaw and was dying slowly and horribly. I didn't much like the woman, but I wouldn't have wished that disease on my very worst enemy.

Phossy jaw – an illness that started with toothache and ended by rotting your face from the inside out. It was common down our way. Two, three women in each street had it. First you lost your teeth. Then you got ulcers, filled with stinking pus. Your face swelled up and rearranged itself into something your own mother wouldn't recognise. If you were lucky, your face got deformed. If you were unlucky, like Mrs Jones, it would eventually kill you. She was already smelling so bad that no one could bear to go sit with her.

And how did you get phossy jaw?

It was easy as pie if you worked in the match factory.

You got it from the phosphorus used to make the matches. It hung in the factory air where Mrs Jones had worked all her life, covering everything with a fine dust.

Phosphorus was pure poison.

But phossy jaw was just one of those things. The danger of getting it came with the job. Same as if you were a docker, like Father, you risked getting injured or drowning in the river every day. Working was dangerous and you had to put up with it. Working was better than starving, and that was the only alternative for the likes of us.

Mother did piece work at home. She got paid by the gross – tuppence for every 144 matchboxes she finished. Me and my sister Nell both had jobs at the match factory. We worked twelve hours a day in winter, fourteen in summer, and we were on our feet the whole time. And there was no getting away from the phosphorus. We breathed it in. We swallowed it down with our dinner. The disease loomed over both of us. We lived in the shadow of phossy jaw, terrified we'd be next.

So why didn't Mr George Arthur Wilkinson do anything about it? The owner of the match factory was a fine upstanding gentleman after all. Didn't he care that he was killing his workers?

Those are very fair questions.

Truth was, we hardly ever got to see the boss. Mr George Arthur Wilkinson would come to the factory maybe once a month for a board meeting or to meet his shareholders. He'd stride past the Prime Minister's statue just outside the gates and come in carrying a silver-topped cane as if it was a truncheon and he knew how to use it. He always had a great big dog with him – a mastiff that looked like it would tear the throat out of anyone who got too close. Mr George Arthur Wilkinson never spoke to any of us and we never spoke to him.

Oh, there had been rumblings and grumblings about phossy jaw from time to time. Once a newspaperman from up west had come to ask him about the disease. But Mr Wilkinson had sworn blind that all his workers were healthy. He said phossy jaw simply didn't exist in his factory. And he was right in a way. Because if anyone got a toothache, the foreman, Mr Fettler, was under orders to say it was a dental problem. And if you had a dental problem, why then of course you'd have to have your teeth pulled. If the disease got worse, Mr Fettler would find any old excuse to kick you out. He'd say a girl was a lazy good-for-nothing, or a troublemaker stirring things up, and she'd get the sack. That was how Mr George Arthur Wilkinson kept his factory "clean and free of the disease".

How could anyone not be angry about that?

But Mother said I needed to calm down. I'd be wanting to get married in a couple of years or so, but what man would ever want me as a wife?

"A husband needs peace and quiet, Eliza," Mother told me. "He needs to be looked after, to feel like he's lord and master in his own home – even if that's just one room in a place like this. A husband will look elsewhere if he can't find comfort with his wife."

It was a useless piece of advice!

Even if Mother had crawled on her hands and knees from one end of Bow Road to the other and begged Father to stay home, he'd still have had his other women. Father had an easy charm, a playful smile and a wandering eye. He could tell a fine tale and dance a merry jig. Women loved him. And he could never resist a pretty face.

Every time Father got caught out with some other woman, he'd come home and beg Mother to forgive him. She'd cry herself dry and then they'd make up and be as happy as honeymooners. Until the next time.

Now, at the ripe old age of fourteen, I'd worked out that Father would have loved Mother more if she'd loved him less. It was a strange lesson to learn. But at least he didn't drink all his wages on a Saturday night and come home reeling, like some of the men in our street. Father didn't beat Mother up and he never laid a hand on his children apart from Jimmy sometimes – and to be fair, Jimmy always deserved it.

I was their first child. Nell had come along a year and a half later. Then there were three boys who all died before they were a year old. After that, Jimmy was born, and he was a barrow load of trouble from the moment he saw the light of day. He got into one scrape after another – he was always up to something. He just couldn't help himself.

Then there were three more girls born one after the other in such rapid succession that they got all lumped together as "the little ones". If they'd ever had names of their own, they never got called by them. I grew up watching Mother tear herself apart with love and loss and worry. She was worn as thin as a thread by the time I was old enough to start working at the factory.

In lots of ways I was an ignorant, uneducated girl. I could barely read or write. Adding and subtracting numbers made me sweat hot and cold all over. But I knew one thing for certain: I did not want to follow in my mother's footsteps. If I was too angry, if my boiling rage put men off?

Then good.

If I lived and died all alone without a husband and family around me?

The peace and quiet would be a blessed relief.

2

It was all noise down our way, a constant deafening uproar. Most of it was horrible to hear. Rats scratching in corners. Beetles scuttling up the walls at night. Dog fights. Catfights. Men brawling. Babies bawling. Women shouting at their children, children yelling at each other. Everyone was always scrapping and crying. Some men, bullied by their bosses during the day, came home at night roaring drunk to take it out on their families. Some Saturday nights, all you could hear were their wives begging for mercy and the children screaming at their father to stop. Sometimes it got so bad that the coppers came along to cart the husband off. And then the wife would be out in the street begging the coppers to leave her husband alone. Because if a man got banged up, his wife wouldn't be able to pay the rent and the family would end up on the streets or in the workhouse. Putting up with a regular beating was better than either of those.

But there was a good kind of noise too. The band playing in the park on a Sunday. Us match girls spilling out of the factory at the end of a shift, laughing and chatting together as we walked home – calling out to fellas, flirting and teasing.

There were a few older women like Ma Lambert who worked at the factory, and a few men. But mostly we were young and full of life. Once a girl was sixteen or maybe seventeen she'd get married and start having babies. And then she'd have her hands so full she'd have to stop working at the factory. We were all planning to have as much fun as we could before that happened.

The best kind of noise was a Saturday, when we only had to work a half-day and we'd get paid. In the evening a big group of us would go up west together to the music hall, or maybe out dancing.

Each week was pretty much the same as the one before. Until one Saturday in June when everything started to change.

I'd been working at the match factory for more than two years by then, but my sister Nell had only started a few months back. I was a cutter and she was a carrier. It should have been the other way round, to tell you the truth, but we had no say in the matter.

I was built like Father: short and stocky and strong. Nell was like a fairy child who'd drifted out of the mist and somehow got trapped in the human world. She seemed not quite here, and that was bewitching. If life had been fair, she wouldn't have been in that factory at all, but like me she never had any choice.

Mr Wilkinson was too tight-fisted to buy trolleys to load the trays of packed matches on to. Nell had to carry them from one place to the other, balancing them on her head and walking careful so as not to spill any. If she dropped even a single box, she got her wages docked.

It was hard work for a little 'un like Nell. After a few months it was already starting to have the same effect on her as it did on all the other carriers. Nell's hair was coming out. At twelve years old, my little sister was going bald.

That particular Saturday Nell was lining up to get paid when she scratched her head. A few strands of hair came away in her hand and Mr Fettler, the foreman, laughed at her. Nell burst out crying and then got docked a whole shilling off her wages for dripping tears on his ledger and making the ink run.

I didn't know any of that until I got home. Nell hadn't waited for me by the gates like she normally did, so I knew something was up. By the time I found her, she was beside herself.

I tried everything I could to cheer Nell up, but nothing worked. I didn't know what to do. Me and her were supposed to be going to the music hall that night with Mary Delaney, who was two years older than me, and Long Tall Sally and Little Jen, who were both the same age as I was. It was our usual gang of girls. But Nell had lost a whole shilling from her pay and now she was saying that she couldn't afford it.

"It's all right, Nell," I said. "I'll treat you."

My sister's eyes lit up for a moment like a struck match, but the fire died just as fast. Her hand went to her head and her eyes suddenly brimmed with tears.

"Tell you what," I said. "You can wear my hat."

3

My hat was a beautiful thing. Big as a cartwheel, with ostrich feathers as long as my arm, dyed scarlet and purple. It had wide satin ribbons tied in great big bows. I'd had my eye on that hat for months before I'd bought it. Anytime we went up west I'd make sure to walk past that particular shop, just to visit the hat, like it was a friend. I'd whisper through the glass at it, "I'm having you one day, my lovely. One day, you're going to be sitting on my head. And won't that be grand, eh? We can go places together, you and me."

I'd lie in bed some nights when I couldn't sleep just imagining walking along Bow Road with the hat on. I'd hold my head high, and the feathers would be dancing with each step I took. I ached for that hat the way some girls ache for their fellas.

We had a fund at the factory. The girls in my section all put a penny in each week and then we drew lots to win it. Week after week, month after month, I prayed to the goddess of hats to pull my name out of it.

And one week she did.

As soon as work finished that Saturday, I was off like a bullet out of the gates, heading straight for that shop.

The woman in there was a right snooty cow. She wouldn't even let me inside till I showed her the coins I was carrying. And after I made my purchase she ushered me out of the door like I was a bad smell. But I had my hat, and with that thing on my head I felt like a queen.

Mother didn't like it of course. She said all the money I'd won from the draw should have gone straight to her so she could put bread on the table for the little ones. Maybe even a bit of meat. But a girl's got to have a treat sometimes, doesn't she? What's the point in living if you can't ever have anything nice?

I kept the hat for special. I'd wear it Saturday nights when me and the other girls headed out. And I'd wear it Sunday afternoons when we went to the park and sat by the pond or listened to the fellas playing on the bandstand. I felt different in that hat, like I was someone special. And I wanted Nell to feel the same.

It was too big for her of course. We had to pack the rim with an old rag to make it fit. But when she had it on and looked in the window glass to see her reflection, the smile that spread across Nell's face was pure gold.

4

We had fun that night at the music hall. There was a man singing a song we hadn't heard before: "Where Did You Get That Hat?" He roared it out, right up to where we were sitting in the cheap seats at the top, looking down on him like we were God almighty. It seemed like his song was meant for me and Nell. We joined in with the chorus and then we sang it all along the Mile End Road on our way home, ignoring people who yelled at us to shut up.

Me and Nell parted from Mary and Sally and Jen at the junction and headed home. We were almost there when this man stepped out of the shadows. He must have been watching us and his eyes were hungry. He was licking his lips like he was going to eat us up.

The man was a toff. Smartly dressed. Black suit, bow tie, cloak. Shoes so shiny they were gleaming even in the dark. Big top hat.

What was a man like that doing in a place like this? Up to no good, I knew that much. I'd seen his kind before.

A year or more ago Molly from down our road had been taken out dancing by a toff like the one standing in front of Nell and me, blocking the path. He'd promised Molly the whole world, got her in the family way, then ditched her. Molly had been as pretty as a picture back then. I'd wanted to be her when I was growing up. But there was nothing pretty left when she was fished out of the Thames drowned and dead. There was no way of knowing whether she'd slipped and fallen or whether she'd jumped.

The toff who was staring at me and Nell struck a match against the wall and lit his cigar. He blew a puff of smoke in our direction, then he threw the match down, grinding it under his heel. And I thought of the factory, and all us girls working our fingers to the bone, and Mrs Jones next door who was dying of the phossy just so this man could light a cigar.

He was watching us the whole time as if me and Nell were objects that belonged to him. All the laughter went out of me and a cold feeling flooded into my chest – so hard and fast it almost knocked me clean off my feet.

I knew this man's type. Never had to do a day's work in his life and wouldn't know how to. Probably couldn't wipe his own behind without a servant doing it for him. He was as useless a human as anyone who'd ever walked the earth. Yet there he was, his eyes crawling over me and Nell. I could see him thinking – no, *knowing* – that he was better than both of us put together.

"What are you looking at?" I said. I couldn't help myself.

"Shhhh!" Nell whispered. "Don't!"

My poor little sister was trembling, but the man didn't bat an eyelid. He looked her up and down and up and down again very slowly, taking in every last detail. He jingled the coins in his pocket. His eyes lingered on the hat and he laughed as if that beautiful thing was amusing. And then he said, "Nothing." He said it very slowly and very deliberately.

Nothing. He said it not like an apology. Like it was a description.

He was looking at me and Nell and we were *nothing*.

How can a man like that make a girl feel dirty without even touching her? I could see Nell didn't feel like a queen any more. She felt like something that had crawled out from under a stone. And so did I.

I broke out in a sweat. I felt hot and cold and shaky all over at the same time. I wanted to say something back. I wanted to crush the man like he'd just crushed Nell, but when I opened my mouth all my words ran away like rats down a sewer. I was so hopping mad that angry tears started to prick the corners of my eyes, but I sure as hell wasn't going to cry in front of him. I didn't want to give him the satisfaction.

"Come on, Nell," I said. And there was a catch in my throat. I grabbed her hand and hurried her away, but somehow I managed to bash her into the wall. The hat slipped off her head and the feathers broke in two. And he saw poor Nell's bald patches and he heard her cry of shame. That man's laughter chased us along the road like a wild animal.

5

The morning after we'd been laughed at by that toff I was in a stinking mood. There was a big black cloud hanging over my head, colouring everything.

I hated Sunday mornings. It was the one full day off we had a week and Mother always ruined it by making us troop along to church. We had to kneel on a cold hard floor, praying to the God who made us poor, giving him thanks for our suffering. I'd never have said it aloud, but I was beginning to think Mother's religion was a load of codswallop. And God didn't strike me down for having that first blasphemous thought, so I began to suspect that maybe, just maybe, I was right. Maybe, just maybe, God didn't exist.

If I'd told Mother that, I'd have been out on my ear, so I had the sense to keep it to myself. But it was hard to button my lip that particular morning.

Father was always allowed to lie in, but Mother started the day by yelling at me to wake up. She and Nell were already getting the little ones ready for church, dressing them in the clothes that Mother had scrubbed to threads the day before. They plaited their hair, gave their faces a good hard wash.

It was my job to deal with my brother, Jimmy. That boy was six years old, three feet tall and ten tonnes of trouble. Jimmy was always up to something. His head was constantly churning with plans and he was always asking questions. Right now he was obsessed with the construction of the new bridge across the Thames. It was going to have two big towers and open up in the middle when ships needed to go upriver. Jimmy had decided that he was going to be an engineer when he grew up and build huge things like that bridge. He'd scurry off to go and watch the men working on it any chance he got.

I'd been like Jimmy once, when I was small. I'd spent hours imagining that when I grew up I'd live in a fine house with an army of servants and have a different hat for every day of the week. But starting at the match factory had knocked all that out of me. Same as it would for Jimmy, in time.

People like us didn't get to choose where we ended up. As soon as Jimmy was old enough, he'd work down the docks like Father. He'd be bribing the foreman with half his wages on a Saturday night just to make sure he'd be given work again the following Monday.

That Sunday I had to get Jimmy clean, but first of all I had to catch him. The little beggar was fast on his feet and out of the door before I had the chance to grab him. Then he was off down the street and I was after him. My legs were twice as long as Jimmy's, so I could run faster. But he had this way of dodging from side to side. Just when I thought I'd got him, I found myself grabbing empty air and falling flat on my face.

He looked back, laughed, and ran slap bang into Mr Jones. The poor man was hobbling up the road from the bath house. Mr Jones walked with crutches. He'd had an accident at the docks a few years back and crushed his leg so badly that half his foot had to be amputated. Now, Mr Jones was thrown against the wall as Jimmy crashed into him and it took him a moment to steady himself.

I grabbed Jimmy by the scruff of his neck and said sorry to Mr Jones. And then I asked after his wife, who was dying of phossy jaw.

He gave me a long sad look. He opened his mouth, but there was nothing to say, so he shut it again and just shook his head.

We both knew Mrs Jones hadn't long to go. And the way she was suffering, death couldn't come soon enough. If I'd been Mother, I'd have promised to pray for her. To pray for them both. I'd have said something comforting. But all I could manage was, "Give her my best ..."

I felt useless as well as angry, and the black cloud hanging over my head grew even bigger.

I turned away and pulled Jimmy back towards the house. "Honest to God, Jim," I said. "I don't know what you do all week to get so filthy. I swear you've got a whole manure heap under your nails."

When we got inside, I said, all cheerful, "Come on, Jimmy." I was hoping that this week we wouldn't have the same performance we'd had every Sunday morning since he started walking.

Jimmy saw dirt the way that most people saw their clothes: he felt naked without a thick layer of muck on him.

You'd have thought I was torturing the lad when it came to washing him. Jimmy wriggled and squirmed, twisting and turning every which way so I couldn't get a proper hold on him. And when I did finally get a good grip, he screamed like I was skinning him alive, not just trying to get him clean.

The noise Jimmy was making woke Father, and Father roared and cursed because he had a splitting headache. But Jimmy didn't stop even when Father came down and gave him a clip around the ear. Or at least he tried to. Jimmy dodged, so I got the whack instead. By the time my little brother looked respectable, I looked as if I'd done ten rounds in a boxing ring. My ears were ringing all morning.

It was so late by then that I couldn't do anything to sort out my own appearance. I had to literally sit on Jimmy to stop him rolling in the gutter until Mother was ready to go. And then I had to keep a firm hold on him all the way to church. Worst of all I had to kneel and pray and when I shut my eyes the face of that toff we'd seen last night was there on my lids. I could see his smug smile and hear his mocking laugh.

How was I supposed to thank God for making us poor and hungry and desperate? How was I supposed to thank God for making that toff rich and fat and so satisfied with himself? I didn't want to pray to God if he'd made the world like that. If God was happy with the way things were, I didn't want nothing to do with him.

6

The church service seemed to last as long as a shift at the factory. The only good thing was the blessed relief when it was finally over. As soon as we spilled onto the street, Jimmy was off. Couldn't see him for dust. He'd find somewhere filthy to roll, and then I'd have the same performance with him next week – on and on and on until one of us keeled over and died.

My thoughts were bitter and bleak, running along dark lines, like a train going into a tunnel. I tried to shake off my mood, but I couldn't.

"We going up the park?" Nell said to me.

My little sister was trying so hard to cheer me up. I smiled at her and said, "Yes. Of course."

So we drifted away from Mother and the little ones and headed off on our own.

"Sorry about the hat," Nell said. "Maybe we could buy new feathers."

But I knew I'd never be able to wear that hat ever again. It was spoilt now. It wasn't just the broken feathers. It was the way that toff had looked at it. Like that beautiful hat was rubbish. Cheap tat. Something to laugh at. But I didn't say that to Nell – there was no point bringing her mood down to my level. Instead I winked and said, "Yes. Things could be worse."

Nell laughed because it was a game we had, just the two of us. We were making fun of Mother in a roundabout way. Mother always said we had to be grateful for what we had, even if what we had was so very little.

"*Wherever you look, there's always someone worse off than yourself,*" Mother would say, like it was a prayer. She repeated it so often that me and Nell had turned it into an act, like the ones you get at the music hall.

I fell into our game right away because Nell was looking at me, waiting.

"Got no coal for the fire, dearie?" I said. "Never mind, eh? At least you got a bed to sleep in."

Nell responded, "No I haven't!"

"Ain't got no bed? You still got the floor, ain't you?"

"But there's no blankets," Nell wailed.

"No blankets?" I exclaimed. "What do you want them for? You've got all those brothers and sisters to keep you warm! Ain't nothing so marvellous as having a family. You should be grateful."

"But we're hungry!" said Nell.

"Ain't you got no money for bread?" I said. "Never mind. At least you still got a roof over your head."

"But I lost my job! I've been thrown out on the street!"

"Well, at least you ain't in the workhouse. Never mind, eh? Could be worse."

"But I am in the workhouse!" Nell protested.

"Oh dear," I said. "That's a shame. Could still be worse. At least you're alive."

"No I ain't."

"You died, did you? Oh dear. What a pity. But at least you didn't die of the phossy."

"Oh yes I did," Nell said.

"Oh."

That's where our little routine ended. Nell and me couldn't imagine anything worse than dying of phossy jaw. It was a dark kind of humour, but me and Nell would laugh at our act sometimes until we almost wet ourselves.

But that day it didn't strike me as being funny any more. It was like that black cloud hanging over me had blotted out the sun. It didn't shift until we got to the park.

And it was there that something happened to change my life for ever.

7

There were always men making speeches in the park. Standing on soapboxes, yelling at anyone who was fool enough to stop and listen.

One fella spent his Sundays screaming, "England for the English!" He was always moaning about immigrants and how they were ruining the place, taking our jobs, driving down wages.

I hated that man. I took it personal, somehow. Nell, Jimmy, the little ones and me were proper Londoners – we'd never been anywhere else. But Father's parents had come to England from Ireland because of the famine and I knew they hadn't felt exactly welcome. If your family were starving, what the hell else were you supposed to do but leave your home? How desperate did you have to be to think the East End of London was some sort of paradise?

I had more sympathy for the man opposite. He spent his Sundays shouting back that immigrants weren't to blame for low wages – it was the bosses' fault. They were taking advantage of the poor and the desperate, setting us all at each other's throats just so they could make more profit.

I knew this man was telling the truth. I'd heard those same things day after day from the other girls. We all moaned about the boss on the way to and from work. But moaning was all we could do.

And the men in the park could say whatever they wanted. It was just a lot of hot air. Empty talk. What was the point of it? Nell and me kept our distance, skirting right around them, heading across the grass.

On a normal Sunday we'd go and sit under the trees by the pond. We might find Jimmy there trying to catch the ducks. Or there'd be a band playing and we'd go and listen and maybe dance. Nell and me would spin across the grass together, laughing our heads off.

If Father wasn't too tired, he'd come along later and bring the rest of the family. When his favourite tune struck up, he'd take Mother in his arms, holding her so close she could hardly breathe. They'd waltz in dizzying circles and

Mother would gaze into Father's eyes like he was the only thing in the world that mattered.

But it wasn't a normal Sunday and I wasn't in the mood for dancing or for sitting by the pond. I wanted to walk, as if by walking I could tame the tangled thoughts that whirled around my head. I had the feeling that if I could get those thoughts into words, and then get the words out of my mouth, the noise inside in my skull would be silenced.

So we walked, Nell and me. And walked. And soon she was puffing and panting and grabbing me by the arm, saying, "Slow down, Eliza! We ain't racing."

I stopped so she could have a bit of a breather and that's when I heard a voice. A woman's. Clear as a bell. High but not shrill. For a moment I thought I'd magicked that voice out of thin air.

"'The rich man in his castle, the poor man at his gate,'" the woman said. "The clergy preach this every Sunday, do they not? They would have us believe that a man's status is determined by God. But can that really be so? Should we accept the way things are? No, I say! I say such things are not decided by the Almighty. I say it is by Man's design that you are born poor. And Man's desire that keeps you in your place."

The woman was well-spoken. A toff. The kind of woman I'd normally avoid like the plague. But I was drawn to her like a moth to a candle flame.

"Where you going now, Eliza?" said Nell. "What you doing?"

I didn't even answer my sister. Suddenly I was running across the grass, without consciously ordering my legs to do it. I joined the crowd who'd gathered to listen to the posh lady speak, pushing my way to the front.

There were men heckling her.

"Go back to your husband, woman!"

"You should be in the kitchen!"

"Ain't you got no shame?"

Some of the men were yelling ruder things than that. But this woman just let it all wash off her, like water off the back of the ducks Jimmy was always after. She kept talking about fairness and justice and workers' rights.

Bang! It was like there was an explosion in my head. Everything was blown apart. And then the pieces came floating back to earth and I could catch my tangled thoughts. I smoothed them straight, pinned them in their place, put them into words.

Mother had always said our lives were hard, but we'd get our reward in the afterlife. Yet I'd never liked the idea of Heaven. Suppose there were toffs there? They'd be sitting on the best clouds, looking down their noses, hogging everything to themselves. I didn't want to spend eternity with them!

Mother said we had to accept our lot in life.

But suppose Mother was wrong? Suppose that this was all there was? Today, now, this moment was the only thing we had.

If that was the case, then we had to change things for the better. No matter how hard it was, no matter how much it cost.

The woman was talking about fairness. Justice. An end to sweatshops and piece work. These things would have seemed like impossible dreams if I'd said them. But this was a toff speaking. An intelligent, educated woman. And despite some people in the crowd grumbling about her being a troublemaker who should go back to where she came from, others were listening and listening hard.

When the woman finished and got down off her soapbox, she smiled my way. For a moment I thought she was looking at me, but then I realised there was a man standing just behind. He was another toff with a great big beard and a smart black suit. He pushed past me and walked towards her, saying, "Wonderful speech."

She took the arm he offered and they walked away together. I was left standing there with my head spinning and my heart pounding so hard against my ribs it was like I'd been dancing a reel.

8

The week that followed was bleeding awful.

Nell cracked a tooth and Father had to pull out what was left of it with a pair of pliers.

My sister didn't make a sound. She didn't cry and she didn't complain. She did what she always did when she was hurt or upset: she retreated right back into herself like a snail in a shell. She was silent as death when we went into work the next day and I couldn't do nothing to get her talking.

I hated it when Nell was like that, so I was in a right old state that morning. Nell's cheek was red and puffy and she kept swallowing down blood from where Father hadn't made a very clean job of it. He'd given Nell a tot of gin to take the pain away but that had made her sick. Her hands were trembling when she loaded the tray of matches on to her head. They trembled so much that she dropped it.

There was a moment of pure silence when time seemed to stop. Everyone in the section froze. They weren't even breathing. We were all staring at those spilled matches, horrified, as if we were staring at the bloodiest of murders. And in a way, we were. Because we all knew what would happen.

Drop one box of matches and you'd get a fine. Drop a whole tray? Mr Fettler, the foreman, would kill Nell. He wouldn't wring her neck, although that might have been kinder. He'd sack her. Then he'd make sure word got around that Nell was clumsy and useless. No one else would ever take her on, so it was as good as killing her, just a slower way of doing it.

I think it was that horrible silence that alerted Mr Fettler to what had happened, not the crash of the dropped tray. He was like a dog smelling blood. A moment before, he'd been nowhere in sight. But then suddenly there he was, grabbing my sister by the arm. He shook her, calling Nell all kinds of names. And then he saw her swollen face and he grabbed hold of her chin and forced her mouth open.

"What's happened to you, girl?" Mr Fettler said.

And Nell didn't say a word. Her eyes were tight shut and I didn't know if she could make sense of what was going on.

I knew that I'd get fined for talking, but I still said, "She cracked a tooth yesterday and Father pulled it. It ain't the phossy, Mr Fettler, honest to God."

Mr Fettler gave me an evil look and said, "All her teeth are rotten. Tell your father he needs to take the lot out. If he does that tonight, I'll let her keep her job. Can't say fairer than that, can I?"

And there was something about the way Mr Fettler was holding my sister that turned my stomach. It was like Nell was something that belonged to him. He could do anything he wanted to her.

I was the only person that could protect Nell. I couldn't keep quiet. "I said it ain't phossy jaw, Mr Fettler. Didn't you hear me? Nell don't need no more teeth taking out."

No one spoke back to Mr Fettler. It was a crime worse than dropping a tray of matches. I'd committed a hanging offence. He let go of Nell and turned to face me.

"What did you say?" Mr Fettler asked.

"She ain't got phossy jaw." My words came out in a whisper.

"Of course she ain't got the phossy!" he said, raising his voice so everyone could hear. "We don't get it here, do we, girls? There ain't never been none in this factory. What are you on about?"

I was standing in the deepest hole and yet I kept right on digging. Mr Fettler probably didn't even remember Mrs Jones, but I said, "My neighbour's dying of it."

"Right gobby little cow, ain't you?" he said. "Do you know what happens to girls who talk back?"

"Yes, Mr Fettler."

"So have you got anything else to say to me?" he said.

"No, Mr Fettler," I replied.

"That's better." He just stood there for a moment or two, staring at me in silence. And then Mr Fettler said, "Take your things and get out."

I felt icy cold. Oh, dear God! He was sacking me. And it was all my fault. What the hell was I going to tell Mother? What would Father say? Without my wages we couldn't pay the rent. We'd all be homeless!

Tears started running down my face. "Don't. Please," I said.

Mr Fettler grinned when he saw me crying. He'd won. I was like a beetle he could crush any time he wanted. Mr Fettler ran his hand down Nell's back. Patted her, like she was his dog.

"I'm in a generous mood," he told me. "You make sure your sister gets all her teeth pulled. Then the pair of you can stay. Otherwise you'll both be out on your ear."

9

Father pulled every tooth out of Nell's head and when it was done she fainted clean away. It took an age to revive her.

When Nell came around, she started crying and I didn't think she'd ever stop. By the morning, she was so ill with fever and pain she couldn't go to work that day or the one after.

Mrs Jones finally died that same week, which was a blessing in a way. But Mother said I had to help her wash the body and lay it out ready for the funeral.

The pair of us dressed Mrs Jones in her Sunday best so she'd look smart when she arrived at the gates of Heaven. I remember thinking that if she stunk as bad up there as she did down here, they'd probably chuck Mrs Jones out. But I didn't say nothing.

I looked at that rotten, ruined face of hers and wondered who'd be next. Me? Nell? Both of us together? It would definitely be someone. And whoever it was would go the same way as Mrs Jones. I hadn't much liked Mrs Jones when she was alive and I was glad her suffering was over, yet I started bawling my eyes out.

When Mr Jones saw me, he thanked me for being a kind, gentle soul, but I wasn't crying for his wife.

I was crying for the rest of us.

10

By the time Monday came around again, I felt broken. Nothing was right. The whole world was a great stinking cesspit of wrong, but there was nothing I could do about it.

Mr Fettler was particularly horrible that day. He kept cornering Nell and looming over me. By the time the pair of us left work that evening I'd never felt so miserable.

But suddenly there was that woman from the park, standing beside the Prime Minister's statue just outside the factory gates, looking like a heavenly vision. She was the woman who'd said we didn't have to put up with the way things were. The woman who'd said things could change for the better if we had the will to act. She was trying to talk to the girls as they poured out into the street, but they were rushing past her like she had leprosy. The woman tried putting a hand on Polly

O'Brien's arm but Polly shook it off and hurried away, running right past me.

"What did she want, Polly?" I called.

"She's stirring things up," said Polly, spitting on the ground. "She wants to talk to someone about what goes on in the factory. I'm not having anything to do with it."

I looked back to where that woman was standing.

"Don't," said Nell, tugging at my sleeve. "Ain't we in enough trouble?"

I don't know what got into me. I saw that woman slump as if she was beaten too, just like I was.

I heard her cry aloud, "Will no one talk to me?"

My voice came out firm and clear.

"Yes," I said. "I will."

11

It wasn't just me who was willing to risk talking to the posh woman. As soon as those words were out of my mouth, others stepped forward. There were five of us: the same gang that me and Nell went up west with on a Saturday night. Mary Delaney, whose workbench was next to mine, Long Tall Sally and Little Jen. We all went along with the posh woman to a place where we could talk.

She was called Mrs Billingham but she told us to call her by her first name: Millicent. Like we were equals. Friends. It felt strange doing that to a toff. Wrong, somehow. Like spitting in church. None of us could quite bring ourselves to do it.

Mrs Billingham said she was a member of a society – a sort of toffs' club – that was campaigning for social justice.

A group of toffs that want things to change? I thought. *Must be a very small club.*

Mrs Billingham had read in the newspaper how much the men who had shares in the match factory were making from them. According to her, they were getting hundreds of pounds in dividends for doing nothing but sit on their fat behinds, while we were working fourteen hours a day for pennies.

She wanted to know what conditions in the factory were like and how badly we were being exploited. She wanted to write about it so people like her would know how bad things were. She wanted things to improve for us.

My sister looked so terrified I thought she'd never get a word out, but the others were bursting to tell Mrs Billingham all they knew. We told her everything.

And to be listened to by a toff and be believed was just ... astounding. It was like Mrs Billingham valued what we had to say – that our opinions, our thoughts, our feelings all counted for something. *We* were something.

It was so different to the way we were normally treated by toffs that it went to our heads. Everything about the factory came flooding out and we were all talking at once, talking over each other. Our words were tumbling and falling over themselves, all so noisy that Mrs Billingham couldn't make head nor tail of what we were saying.

"One at a time," she said, her hands up as if she was defending herself. "Please. I can't take it in."

So we took turns.

Mary talked about how her mother had worked in the match factory when things hadn't been so bad. "Back then the old boss was running the show," Mary said. "He was a Quaker who tried to treat the girls fairly. By the time I started, his son had taken over. He changed his religion, from Quaker to Church of England. But you know what he really worships? Wealth. Profit. I get paid less and work longer hours than my mother did twenty years ago! How can that be right?"

Then Sally said that in her mother's time there was a dinner hall at the factory, where you could eat whatever scraps of food you'd managed to bring from home. Phossy jaw hadn't been so common then because whatever you ate wasn't covered in phosphorus.

"But the new boss, young Mr Wilkinson, thought it took too long for girls to leave their sections and troop along to the dinner hall," said Sally. "So he changed all that. We have to eat at our workbenches now. We get a nice, tasty sprinkling of phosphorus with every meal!"

I told Mrs Billingham about Mr Fettler and his thieving, bullying ways. After a nod from Nell, I told her about Nell's teeth and how it was Mr Fettler's fault she'd had to have the whole lot pulled. I said how close we'd come to losing our jobs a week ago and how he'd hold that threat over our heads for ever. He'd keep us bowing and scraping and saying, "Yes, Mr Fettler, no, Mr Fettler, three bags full, Mr Fettler. Can I kiss your behind now, Mr Fettler?"

Then Nell finally found her voice and she said, all timid, "We've had enough, ain't we, Eliza?"

"We have, Nell," I said. "More than enough."

"And is it just the five of you that think this way?" Mrs Billingham asked. "Or do the rest of the match girls feel the same?"

"It's all of us!" said Mary. "Everyone's been raging for years. But there's nothing we can do about it. Apart from that one time – do you remember the statue?" Mary looked around at the four of us.

The statue! Who could forget? The incident had happened before any of us had started working at the match factory, but we knew the story off by heart. We could picture it in our heads as clear as a real memory, so we told it to Mrs Billingham as if we'd been there.

"You'll have seen the Prime Minister's statue by the factory gates, Mrs Billingham," I said. "It was the boss who decided to put that up. Only he didn't pay for it. We did."

"Some of us only earn four shillings a week, Mrs Billingham," Nell said.

"Less after Mr Fettler has dipped his hand into our pockets!" said Sally.

"But do you know what he did?" said Mary. "Mr Wilkinson took a whole shilling from every single one of us to pay for that bleeding statue."

"And do you know what else?" said Jen. "He closed the factory for half a day so we could all go along and watch the damned thing being unveiled. Mr Wilkinson called it a holiday, but it meant we lost half a day's pay on top of the shilling."

"But we weren't having that, were we?" Mary said. "The day of the statue's unveiling we were all hopping mad. We trotted along to that ceremony with bricks in our pockets and rotten eggs and whatever else we could find lying in the gutter."

"We paid for that statue, so why shouldn't we have some fun with it?" said Sally.

Jen was laughing now. "After the ceremony," she said, "we pelted the Prime Minister's statue until it was covered in stinking muck."

Mary finished the story. "And old Ma Lambert got so flaming angry she scratched her arms until they bled. She hitched up her skirts and climbed up on to the plinth and wiped the statue's hands until they were dripping red. Then she yelled, 'We paid for it with our lifeblood. Now everyone can see the truth!'"

We talked and talked until Mrs Billingham couldn't listen to any more. I'm sure we could have kept on talking for days, but we'd worn her out.

Mrs Billingham was going to publish our story in her society newsletter. But she said she wouldn't mention any of us by name so we wouldn't get in trouble.

I'd never heard of the newsletter and no one I knew ever read anything. I thought that would be the end of it.

I thought wrong.

12

"Gobby little cow!"

A week later Mr Fettler was shouting in my face. He was so close I could smell his breath. And that smell did something to me. It took me back to being twelve years old again. Just starting work at the factory. Faint with terror.

It took a while for me to notice that he was waving a piece of paper at me. It took even longer to realise it was Mrs Billingham's newsletter.

She hadn't mentioned our names, but she'd written down exactly what I'd told her about Nell's teeth and our foreman. It was all laid out there in black and white type. It was as plain as day who'd talked to her.

"Gobby little cow!" Mr Fettler said again. Only this time he spat it out and droplets of his spittle hit my cheeks. "Go squealing to her, did you? Well, you ain't getting away with it."

All the courage, all the excitement, all the relief I'd felt when we were talking to Mrs Billingham melted away. Any hope of a better future slid down the drain before my very eyes.

My head pounded. I felt sick to the stomach. I was dizzy with the stupidity of what I'd done. I was going to lose my job. And no one would ever take me on anywhere else because what employer would take on a known troublemaker? I'd end up starving on the streets.

I thought I was going to faint. I may have looked that way too, because suddenly Mr Fettler grabbed the front of my dress and shook me so hard my teeth rattled.

"It's all lies," he said. "You got to say it was all lies. You got to say you're happy in your work, understand me? You got to say you're well paid and well looked after."

Who does he want me to talk to? I thought. *What am I supposed to say?* I knew it wouldn't make any difference if I went and begged Mrs Billingham to say it was all a mistake. She knew the truth now and she wasn't the kind who'd turn her back on it.

That was when I saw Mr Fettler had a second piece of paper besides Mrs Billingham's newsletter.

Words were already written on it. He laid it down on my workbench. I wasn't a fast reader at the best of times and now my head was spinning and the words were dancing on the page. I could make out the name Mrs Billingham. And then there were other words that didn't make sense.

"It says your friend Mrs Billingham is a radical socialist who invented the whole story for political reasons of her own," Mr Fettler said. "It says she's manipulating you. Tricking you into saying things that aren't true. Sign it. And then you and your sister can keep your jobs."

There was a deathly hush. All the girls in my section were watching, motionless. Sally had her hands clasped over her mouth. Mary's arms were folded across her bosom. Jen's jaw was clenched tight. The only sound was a fly banging against the window. I could see Nell out of the corner of my eye, standing on the steps, frozen still.

I didn't have any choice. I'd never had any choice. Things were as they were. I had to accept that.

I watched Mr Fettler dip the pen in the inkwell. He held it out to me and I took it. My hand was hovering over the paper.

I didn't think I believed in God any more, but maybe he was trying to prove me wrong, because what happened next felt like divine intervention.

I seemed to fly out of my own body. Suddenly, I was up there on the ceiling, looking down at the factory floor. I could see myself below – a hollow, empty shell of a girl – and Mr Fettler looming over me.

And then, clear as clear, I could see exactly what would happen next. It all unfolded before my eyes as if I was in a music hall, sitting up in the cheap seats, watching actors on stage.

I saw myself signing that paper. I saw the grin on Mr Fettler's face and the way he pulled himself up as if he was the most mighty man on earth. I could see him delighting in the power he had over me.

I saw him getting all the other girls to sign the paper, one by one.

And then I saw Mr Fettler sacking me and Nell just because he could. Just because he wanted to grind us into the dirt. To teach us a lesson. To prove to all the other girls that he was in charge and he could make each and every one of them suffer like me and my sister.

Then with a BANG! I was back at my workbench, looking up at Mr Fettler as he waited for me to sign.

But I must have looked at him different, because he frowned.

I knew now that whatever I did, I'd lose my job. But if I signed that thing, I'd lose something worse. I'd lose any hope of changing things for the better. I'd lose my last shreds of self-respect. And I'd lose all my dignity.

For the very first time, I looked Mr Fettler straight in the eye.

I had nothing whatsoever to lose. Suddenly, I felt free as a bird.

"No," I said.

And that one word, though quietly spoken, was like a cannon going off.

Shockwaves rolled across the factory floor.

There was such a sharp intake of breath from the other girls that they must have sucked up all the air for a moment, because Mr Fettler gasped and turned red.

Slowly, deliberately, I laid down the pen. Slowly, deliberately, I picked up that piece of paper. Slowly, deliberately, I ripped it in two.

And then fourteen years of rage came pouring out of my mouth. And this time I didn't cry angry, frustrated tears. This time the words didn't trip and fall over each other. This time they took to the air like starlings. A beautiful flock of words flying around that factory floor.

"I ain't signing nothing," I said. "I know damned well you'd sack me after, because nothing you ever say or do is honest. You're a liar and a cheat and a bully, Mr Fettler, and I ain't having it no more. You know as well as I do that everything Mrs Billingham wrote in that newsletter is God's honest truth. And we didn't even tell her the half of it."

Mr Fettler had gone deathly pale, as if my words had wounded him.

Good.

"Get out," he said.

"I'm going," I replied. "But you ain't sacking me. I'm walking out. Leaving of my own free will. You can take your job and shove it where the sun don't shine. You don't own me, Mr Fettler. You don't own none of us. You're a pile of filthy rubbish. But I am something. I am someone. And I've had enough!"

It seemed the entire world was in shock. There was silence.

Broken by a voice. Nell's.

"And me. I'm coming with you," she said. Slowly, deliberately, my sister was taking the tray off her head. She held it in her hands. Slowly, deliberately, she lifted it up to her chin. And then, slowly and deliberately, she dropped it on the floor.

Crash!

And then it was like being at the music hall. People were laughing, clapping. Cheering.

Cheering us. Giving me and my sister a round of applause like we'd done something to be proud of. And we had. We had!

When me and Nell walked out of the factory, fourteen hundred match girls followed.

13

"Walking out? Starting a strike? Unplanned?
Unprepared? What were you thinking, Eliza?"
Mother was appalled at what me and Nell had
done.

And when Father came home, he hit the roof
too. "Don't you know that no strike has ever
succeeded?" he roared. "Haven't you learned
by now that the bosses hold all the cards? Mr
Wilkinson just has to sit on his fat arse and wait.
He knows perfectly well that come rent day, all
the girls will come crawling back with their tails
between their legs. How are we going to manage
without your wages? And without Nell's?"

"We'll get by," I said, still giddy with the
excitement of what had happened that day. "We'll
work something out."

But Mother said I'd done the most stupid thing
anyone in the family had ever done. And seeing

as we lived with Jimmy, who was always up to something stupid, that took some doing.

I couldn't put it into words, but I knew that Mother and Father were wrong to think that the strike was unplanned. In a funny way I'd been planning it my whole life. I just hadn't realised until it happened. I could see now that everything I'd ever done, everything I'd ever thought and felt, had been leading up to this moment. All my anger, all my rage – I finally had something to pour it into. It had a target. A use. So I let Mother's mumbling and Father's grumbling wash over me.

I went to bed that night with a smile on my face and hope in my heart. I crushed the doubts Mother and Father had planted in my head. I ignored the rumbling belly that warned me we'd be starved into submission before the week was out. Me and Nell lay side by side and waited until Jimmy and the little ones were fast asleep. Then we whispered about what might happen tomorrow.

We were planning to head up west.

Me and Nell and the usual gang were going to find Mrs Billingham. She had a right to know what had happened.

And when she heard about the strike, she'd help us. She had to.

After Nell drifted off to sleep, I lay in the dark staring up at the ceiling. It was a long time before I slept, but when I did, for some strange reason I dreamed about my hat.

14

First thing the following morning we set out to find Mrs Billingham. I'd had the sense to snatch the newsletter out of Mr Fettler's hand when I'd walked out of the factory the day before. He'd been standing there, bewildered. Speechless for the first time in his life.

It was just as well I'd grabbed that newsletter because there was an address at the top of the first page that I thought must be her office. We'd never have known where to look for Mrs Billingham otherwise.

When we started out, it was just the five of us who'd spoken to her. But word had got around and, as we walked along the Mile End Road, more and more girls joined us. By the time we got up west there were hundreds of us marching arm in arm right up the middle of Fleet Street.

Traffic had to get out of our way. We caused such a jam!

There were bystanders either side of the road who wanted to know what was going on and what all the commotion was about. Some of them looked disapproving but more were whooping and cheering and yelling their support.

"Courage, ladies!"

"God speed!"

"Good luck!"

Even the coppers who were sent to clear us out of the way were on our side. They re-directed the traffic so we had the street to ourselves. Nell and me were riding the crest of a wave and it felt marvellous.

Luck was running our way because Mrs Billingham was at her office when we arrived. She invited a group of us inside. When we were all crammed in together, we told her what we'd done.

And Mrs Billingham was as appalled as Mother had been.

"A strike?" she said, suddenly sitting down as if she might be about to swoon. "Oh my goodness! Isn't that a little ... drastic?"

"What were you expecting?" I asked her. "When you wrote about us, you must have hoped something would happen."

"I thought maybe it would lead to a boycott," she said. "I was hoping to persuade people not to buy your particular brand of matches."

Mary laughed as if Mrs Billingham had made a joke. "What bleeding good would that have done?" she asked.

"I thought if sales were reduced, then Mr Wilkinson might be persuaded to improve conditions," Mrs Billingham replied.

Jen said, "If the boss started losing sales, who do you think would pay for it? It wouldn't be him, that's for sure. He'd just cut our wages to make up the difference."

"But a strike!" Mrs Billingham said. "To withhold your labour ..."

"Our labour is the only weapon we've got," said Sally. "Walking out was the only way to make Mr Wilkinson listen."

"But how will you live?" Mrs Billingham asked. "How will you feed yourselves?"

There was a moment or two of silence. All the doubts and the whispers that I'd held at bay came

rushing in. Because how *were* we going to get by?
We were beaten before we'd even got started.

I felt a pain behind my eyeballs – the sure sign
of a headache coming on. I closed my lids and
rubbed them. An image of my hat came into my
mind, just as it had last night. My glorious, ruined
hat.

Paid for by the fund.

My eyes snapped open. "My hat, Mrs
Billingham!" I said. She looked at me as if I'd gone
mad, but I carried on. "I bought a great big hat
once. I'd never have been able to afford it on my
own. But we've got a fund, see? Each girl in our
section puts in a penny and then we have a draw
at the end of the week. Suppose we do something
like that now? This society of yours … How many
members have you got?"

"Several hundred," Mrs Billingham said.

So I said, "And are they all as wealthy as you?"

"Oh yes," she said.

And I said, "Do they really want to see things
change?"

She bristled a bit at that, as if I was implying
that they might be all talk and no action.

She said, "They're deeply and sincerely
committed to the Socialist cause."

I slapped my hand on her desk, triumphant. "Well, then," I said. "How about your members put their money where their mouths are? If they all chipped in just a little bit, we could have a fund for any match girl who's in difficulty, couldn't we?"

"It would need to be organised …" Mrs Billingham began, but trailed off. She was struggling to understand how it might work. Talking and writing was one thing. But actually doing something was altogether different. Like all toffs, Mrs Billingham wasn't used to getting her hands dirty. But we were. Getting organised and looking out for each other was something we knew inside out. We did it all day, every day.

"Could you write something about it in your newsletter?" I asked. "Put out an appeal?"

Mrs Billingham brightened. "Yes … Yes! Of course I could!"

"There will be others too," Nell piped up. "Working people. People like us. Look at how those shop girls reacted when we came here, spilling out into the street. All them delivery boys and cabbies and flower sellers clapping and cheering us on. Even the coppers! There were hundreds of them. If they all just put in a penny or two each, it would make a difference."

"A strike fund," Mrs Billingham said. She had the bit between her teeth now and was raring to go. "I'll get started right away."

"And we'll make a list of people who'll need help," I said. "We'll hold a meeting and tell the girls what's going on."

Unplanned? Unprepared?

No!

I'd show Mother and Father they were wrong about that.

I'd show everyone.

15

We held our meeting at Mile End Waste ground. It was what you might call "lively". Fourteen hundred girls were gathered, all with opinions as firm and voices as loud as my own. And all with different ideas about what we should do next. Some were already fretting about having lost two days' pay and wanted to go back to work. But most of us were ready to stick it out and it was our voices that were the loudest, for now at any rate.

Mrs Billingham had said we should draw up a list of demands. Things that needed doing by the boss before we'd return to work. It was the proper way to organise a strike, she told us. But it was easier said than done.

To begin with, it was mayhem, with everyone shouting out suggestions at the same time. But then someone – Mary, I think – said we should form a strike committee. The five of us who'd talked to Mrs Billingham should be on it. And then each section from the factory should pick one girl to represent the others.

Well, that took most of the morning, but at last we had ourselves a committee of around forty girls. We put old Ma Lambert in charge of it, the woman who'd once bloodied the Prime Minister's statue. She'd raised six strapping sons, all of them dockers. If Ma Lambert could keep them in order on a Saturday night with just a look, keeping us girls in line would be a doddle. But even with her running things it took us most of the afternoon to come up with a list of demands that we were all happy with.

When we put it to the rest of the girls, some said we'd gone too far. Others said that we hadn't gone far enough. But we all agreed things couldn't go on the way they had before.

Next, we had to start a strike register, which was a list of everyone who might need help from the strike fund.

Half the girls were too proud to take what they saw as charity. It was the start of the hop-picking season in Kent, so they said they'd head down there to find work. That still left seven hundred or more who'd need help with rent and food. Nell wrote the list while I sat watching her. She was a marvel, my sister. I always struggled to make those letter shapes on paper, but it came as easy as breathing to Nell.

By the end of that day we'd got ourselves organised, which impressed Mrs Billingham no end. We were a force to be reckoned with, she said. If the boss had any sense at all, he'd roll over and give us what we wanted right away.

But Mr George Arthur Wilkinson was a rich and powerful man. He wasn't going to give in without a fight. And he didn't mind fighting dirty.

The very next day, Mr Wilkinson declared he'd sue Mrs Billingham for libel.

Well, that threat was just a load of hot air. There were seven hundred match girls still in London who were prepared to stand up in a court of law and swear every line in Mrs Billingham's newsletter was God's honest truth. So Mr Wilkinson resorted to other means. Filthy, underhand means.

He had a friend who owned a newspaper and that week they started to spread lies about us. The story on the front page talked about us poor, ignorant match girls being used as pawns in a political game. It said that we had been cruelly cheated by Mrs Billingham and her Socialist comrades. The newspaper said we were being manipulated by Radical Left Wingers for their own revolutionary purposes.

"Cheek of it!" I said, after Nell had read it aloud for all of the committee to hear. "What do they think we are? Sheep? Being herded wherever Mrs Billingham wants us to go?"

"They've got a bloody nerve!" said Nell. And then she blushed because she'd sworn for the first time in her life.

Old Ma Lambert hitched up her bosom like she was readying herself for battle. The sight of her almost made me laugh, because the idea of anyone trying to tell her where to go or what to do was just plain ridiculous. She said, "We'd best prove them wrong then, hadn't we?"

"How are we going to do that, Mrs Lambert?" said Mary.

"We show them the truth," Ma Lambert said. "We let them see who we are and what we're made of."

"Yes," I said. "We show everyone we've got minds of our own. That we're doing this for ourselves, not because some toff is leading us astray."

"But how?" said Nell.

And old Ma Lambert and Sally and me all spoke at the same time.

"We march."

*

We marched every single day. Some of us marched barefoot. The rest of us were in boots with soles so thin it was hardly worth the bother of putting them on. All of us were as skinny as rakes and wearing threadbare dresses but we marched. Hundreds of us walking miles and miles around the streets of London. What a sight it was! We carried placards and banners that Jimmy had scraped together out of nothing. My brother was in his element finding bits and pieces of rubbish, fixing them together, writing slogans with paint he'd begged from God-alone-knows where. We chanted chants, we rattled buckets for the strike fund, we demanded justice. It was so exciting! Even better than the best of Saturday nights.

Being one of a crowd makes you feel bigger. Better. I was one small person, and yet I could feel a power within me that week that grew and grew until I felt like I could defeat dragons. I could take on – take down – anyone at all. It must be how men get when they go marching off to war. Comrades in arms. Brothers. Well, we were sisters, tied as tight together as men in battle. And we were fighting an enemy that was as deadly as any invading army.

16

At the end of the strike's first week we had a rally in Hyde Park. Mrs Billingham got up to address the gathered crowd.

"These helpless, hapless girls are the victims of a cruel and ruthless employer," Mrs Billingham began. "He holds them in his iron fist and crushes them at will."

It was a strange thing. I'd loved hearing her in the local park that first time. But now the more Mrs Billingham talked and the posher she sounded, the less sympathy there was for us amongst the gathered crowd. I could feel their support ebbing away, and I didn't know what to do.

In a blinding flash I suddenly saw that Mrs Billingham was talking about us in the same way the newspaper had – as if we were mindless sheep caught between two opposing sides, blindly running around with no will of our own. Mrs

Billingham hadn't meant to of course, but she was proving that what the newspaper said was true.

"They need to hear it from one of us," I said to Nell.

"They need to hear it from you," she said.

"Me?" I said.

"Ain't you the girl who told Mr Fettler where he could stick his job?" said Mary, who was standing on the other side of Nell.

And the next thing I knew I was up on the platform.

I don't know how I got there. I think it was Mary and Sally who pushed me up. One minute I was amongst the crowd, the next I was looking down on them.

And I didn't have a single clue of what to say.

Mrs Billingham had stood aside and was waiting for me to begin. I gawped like a fish out of water for what seemed like an eternity. I looked at that crowd. All those faces.

Match girls. Strangers. Because it wasn't just us. It was them too. I could see toffs. And I could hear their thoughts as clearly as if they'd shouted them aloud.

Ugly, common creature!

Vulgar little thing!

There was a man in a top hat looking at me like I was nothing. I don't think it was the same man who'd laughed at me and Nell that Saturday night, but he was cut from the very same cloth.

But there were other people in that crowd who were egging me on. Old Ma Lambert. Sally. Jen. Mary. Nell. The faces of neighbours. Friends. People who struggled to get by. I was doing this for them. For us.

So I started speaking.

"Mrs Billingham – bless her!" I said. "She wants to help us and don't think I'm not grateful for that because I am. But all of us here know Mrs Billingham can go home at the end of the day and she can have a nice big dinner and climb into a nice warm bed. She can shut her eyes at night and she won't have to lie there on a hard floor, listening to her belly rumbling and beetles scuttling up the wall. She doesn't have to live it, not like I do. I live it every single day, and I can tell you God's honest truth.

"The newspaper said our minds have been turned by the Socialists," I went on. "That we've been led astray.

"That's a bunch of lies. We're here because we want to be. Mrs Billingham didn't start this. I did.

Me and my sister walked out and the rest of the girls followed. We did it of our own accord. And you know why? Because we've had enough.

"We've had enough of being bullied by a thieving foreman. We've had enough of having our wages docked for no reason. We've had enough of seeing our mothers, our sisters and our friends die of phossy jaw. We've had enough of the boss lying about it, saying it doesn't exist. We've had enough of being terrified every minute of every day that we'll be next, and being scared witless every time one of us gets a toothache.

"Some of you are looking at me and seeing a skinny little match girl. You're wondering who the hell I think I am, getting up here and daring to talk to you lot? I can see you thinking it, over there, missus. Yes – you in the purple dress with your arms folded. You think I should stay in my place, don't you? And you, sir." I pointed to the toff. "Standing there in your top hat, smoking your cigar, thinking I'm a scruffy little urchin with no right to be here. I've got a flaming nerve, haven't I?

"Well, you're right, sir," I continued. "I have got a flaming nerve. And so has every single match girl in the factory. We've all got hearts and minds and souls that are just as good as yours. And we are standing up for ourselves. We are going to yell from the rooftops until everyone in this city hears us. We demand to be treated fair. And this time, this time we will succeed. We will win this.

"I'm just one person. What can one person do, eh? Well, maybe one person can't do much, no more than one drop of water can be a flood. But if there are hundreds, thousands of drops all joining together? Then you get a river as big as the Thames. And we all know that when the tide turns, there's nothing on earth that can resist that river. As long as we stay united in this struggle, we will be unstoppable.

"Who's with us?" I finished.

Judging from the cheering and the roaring, everyone in Hyde Park was. All apart from the toff, who turned on his heel and left.

17

When Nell and me walked home that night, we were flying as high as kites.

But the moment we rounded the corner into our street I knew something was wrong. When we got inside the house, Nell and me came crashing down to earth.

Father never came home before dark, but now he was sitting by the empty grate, staring into it, not seeing anything. My father looked broken, no longer the charmer who never let anything get him down. There was a hush so thick I thought someone had died. Accidents happened at the docks all the time, so I thought maybe one of his mates had been killed.

"What's the matter?" I whispered to Mother.

She gave me such a look. She didn't have to say it. Whatever had happened was clearly my fault.

"There was no work for him today," Mother said.

I knew what the words meant, but I couldn't take them in.

"No work?" I echoed stupidly.

"No. Work."   .

I couldn't understand it. Father had always worked down at the docks. He took care to keep in with the foreman and slip him a few shillings every Saturday.

But now suddenly Father had been sent home.

I knelt at his feet and said, "What happened?"

It took a while for Father's eyes to focus and even longer for him to reply. He smiled at me, or at least he tried to. His usual playful grin was just a shadow of itself.

Whenever Father was upset or excited, his accent got stronger. It was as thickly Irish as I'd ever heard it when he said, "It's not your fault. Don't you go blaming yourself."

But I did. Of course I did.

Father said his foreman had asked after Nell and me right before he'd said there wasn't any work. Mr George Arthur Wilkinson couldn't get to me or Nell directly, so he'd used his influence over other employers in the city. He was hurting my father to get to me and my sister.

And there was nothing we could do about that.

"He can't get away with this!" I said.

"He can and he will," Mother replied. She was in such a fury, seeing Father in that state, and she took it all out on me. "There's no fighting Mr Wilkinson, Eliza. He's too powerful. You were a fool to even try."

All those marvellous words I'd had in the park vanished. I couldn't talk to Mother about rivers and tides when we were standing in a house we couldn't afford to rent any more. The strike fund might cover me and Nell's wages, but we couldn't expect it to cover Father's. We were homeless. The thing we'd always dreaded had happened. And I was to blame.

Father said he'd take Mother and Jimmy and the little ones down to Kent to pick hops. That would give them work for a week or two, at any rate.

He said, "Come with us, Eliza. Let things cool off a bit, eh? The match girls can manage without you, can't they?"

Father had never asked me to do anything before then. Not one single favour. And there was something in that request and his sad smile and his broken look that made me weaken.

The word "yes" formed on my lips, but before it could slip out Nell put a hand up to my mouth.

"Eliza can't leave," Nell said, turning to our parents. "You should have seen her today. She was like a queen, telling everyone what for. They wouldn't listen to Mrs Billingham. But they listened to Eliza. She can't go. She just can't. If Eliza goes, we'll lose and we'll never stop losing. She's staying here to fight. And I'm staying with her."

18

The next morning, Nell and I stood watching Father load the little ones up on a borrowed barrow. Mother was so upset she could barely bring herself to speak to us, but Father was more forgiving.

"You're brave girls, the pair of you," he said. "Daughters a man can be proud of. I wish you luck."

Father kissed us both and took hold of the handles of the barrow.

Jimmy suddenly rushed at me, his arms out. He flung them so tightly around my waist I thought he'd break my spine.

"You be a good boy now, Jimmy," I said, ruffling his hair, noticing the grime behind his ears. How long would it be before I had to scrape him clean on a Sunday again? My voice cracked a bit when I added, "You come back home to me safe, eh? And when you do, we'll take you up west, Nell and me.

We can go look at the new bridge, eh? See how those towers are getting on."

Nell and me were left behind to finish what we'd started. We'd been strong while the family were in front of us, but the moment they vanished around the corner we both burst into tears. We stood in the street clinging to each other. Mother and Father, the little ones and Jimmy had left holes in our hearts as big as craters.

Those first few days of the strike had been so exciting. But now the grim reality hit me and Nell like a brick to the head.

We went to stay with Mary. There were thirteen of us in one room, packed like sardines in a tin, and not enough food to go around. We had the strike fund, but it had to be used for seven hundred girls. The money was already dwindling fast and no matter how generous people were, we couldn't go on like this for ever.

As the days passed, things got more and more tense. We carried on with the marching and the speech making, but desperation was creeping in.

One morning old Ma Lambert arrived at the start of a committee meeting saying she'd heard a rumour that the boss was planning to ship girls down from Glasgow to fill our places. She didn't know where the story had started or who'd first heard it. It might have been pure nonsense. But it still struck fear into our hearts.

"What do we do if that happens?" said Mary.

"We talk to them," I said. "The Glasgow girls. We ask them to walk out too. In solidarity. We join forces."

"You think they'd listen?" said Jen.

"Why not?" I said. "We're all in the same boat, ain't we? More or less?"

"And what if the boss ships in girls from other places?" said old Ma Lambert. "Immigrants who don't speak English? You think you could persuade them to stand with us too?"

"There would be a way," I said. And I sounded so sure of myself, but inside I was shaking.

"You can't bring the whole world out on strike Eliza," said Mary.

Old Ma Lambert just shook her head and said nothing.

*

The next day we heard a rumour that was even worse. People said Mr Wilkinson was thinking of moving the whole factory abroad, where workers were cheaper. If that happened, fourteen hundred match girls would be out on their ears, and with jobs so hard to come by we'd end up fighting each other for whatever we could get. Girls were already whispering that we should throw in the towel and go back to work right now to prevent that disaster.

"It's just a rumour," I told them. "That's all. Mr Wilkinson's trying to scare us into giving in. But we can't. We mustn't. If we let him win now, he'll never stop punishing us."

Brave words, eh? But I wasn't convincing anyone, least of all myself. I knew that the strike couldn't go on much longer. Yes, my words were big and bold and when I addressed the crowds they cheered and roared their support, but I had the nagging feeling that it all might come to nothing. The boss could wait for as long as it took to break us. And then we'd have to go back to the factory on whatever terms he offered, because when it came down to it, any job was better than nothing, no matter how badly paid. No one would willingly starve if there was anything they could do to stop it.

One night I found myself praying to the God I didn't believe in that when the strike did end, it would end in our favour.

And maybe God really did exist after all, because the very next day there were letters in the newspaper from people who'd seen the state of us. They'd noticed how skinny we were, how some girls had to walk barefoot because they couldn't afford shoes. They'd heard the truth from our own lips and listened to me talk about phossy jaw. The people who wrote the letters were important and powerful and wealthy. They were toffs. The kind of people that Mr George Arthur Wilkinson wanted to be on the right side of.

All the time we'd been marching and making speeches, Mrs Billingham and her friends had been busy on our behalf. They'd written letters, articles, addressed toffs' meetings, talked to other people like themselves. And by a miracle of miracles, they'd managed to persuade some Members of Parliament to meet us and listen to what we had to say. A couple of days later, me, Nell, the usual gang and the rest of the girls on the strike committee found ourselves setting off to Westminster and the Houses of Parliament.

19

The Houses of Parliament! It was the most
frightening place I'd ever seen. So big. So grand.
It was like being in a cathedral with echoing
corridors, vaulted ceilings and portraits of toffs
whose eyes followed you wherever you went. It
was meant to make the likes of me feel small, I
thought. And it worked. I was shrivelling into a
shell, same as Nell was.

We got into the committee room and that
feeling got even worse. It wasn't like when the
five of us had talked to Mrs Billingham, our stories
pouring out, getting all mixed and muddled in
their haste to be told. Here there was a system
that needed to be followed. A formal way of doing
things. Organisational procedure. An agenda.
Minutes taken. All written down for the record.
When the officials got started, it was like hearing

people talking in a foreign language. I couldn't make head nor tail of it.

According to Mrs Billingham, some of the MPs we were meeting were sympathetic to our cause. But others weren't. And, as luck would have it, I got questioned by one who was as unsympathetic as any man could be.

The other girls had been asked about the goings on at the factory and what their lives were like, how much they got paid, how long the shifts were, that kind of thing.

But then it was my turn. And this unsympathetic man pulled his spectacles down his nose and peered over them at me. And he began to ask me a question so long, with so many twists and turns and so many big, baffling words, that by the time he got to the end of it I couldn't remember what the beginning had been.

When I didn't answer, the man just sat, tapping his fingernails on the table, staring at me in silence like I was something that had crawled out of a sewer.

My temper started to bubble up, warming me from the inside, pouring courage into my veins.

I said, "Mr whatever-your-name is, let me tell you something. My father works down the docks.

And sometimes he doesn't speak English to his mates, he speaks Irish instead. He does it so the foreman won't understand what he's saying. It's like a secret code. And I reckon you've got a code here too. You talk in sentences that turn so many corners anyone listening gets lost in them. You use words so big they won't fit in anyone else's mouth. You try to confuse people like me who don't know the code. You try to make them feel small and stupid.

"I haven't got a clue what you just asked me," I went on, "but then I wasn't supposed to understand, was I? You were just making yourself look clever by making me look stupid. You wanted it to seem like we're not worth your time and your consideration. Well, I might not have your education, but I reckon I've got a mind that's as nippy as yours. So how about we have ourselves an agreement? You talk plain English to me and I won't talk Irish at you."

I smiled brightly then, and the MPs that were sympathetic to our cause chuckled and one even said, "Hear, hear!"

Mr whatever-his-name-was shuffled his papers. And then he asked, "Does your family struggle financially?"

"Yes," I said.

And he said, "What does your father do?"

And I said, "I already told you. He works down the docks."

So he said, "Does he get regular work?"

And I said, "He has done until now."

He sat back in his chair, put his fingertips together and looked up at the ceiling. "Let me get this right. If I understand you correctly, your father gets paid several shillings a week. That should be sufficient for your family's needs. With the wages you and your sister bring in you should be perfectly comfortable. Why are you struggling financially? Does your father bring home all he earns?" He leaned forward and then asked, "Or does he drink it?"

It was like a slap around the face. I flinched. "No, he doesn't," I said.

"Gambles it away, maybe?"

I was raging now. I said, icy cool, "No."

There was a long pause. And then I said, "You want to know why my family struggle? It's because every time Father gets paid on a Saturday he has to slip almost half his wages to the foreman just to ensure he'll get work again on Monday. If he doesn't do that, he'll be there outside the gates every single morning, one of six hundred men fighting for maybe six jobs. And I mean really fighting. It gets ugly down there. So, no, my father doesn't bring home all he earns. And neither do I and neither does my sister, because our foreman's dipping his hand into our pockets too. But none of us are feckless, I assure you."

"And your mother works too, does she?" the man asked.

"Mother has Jimmy and the little ones to mind," I replied, "but she does piece work, making matchboxes. The children get put out to play in the street in all weathers so she can spread the boxes out over the floor to dry. She gets paid tuppence a gross. And she has to pay for her own glue and her own brushes out of that. She works all the hours of daylight and she brings in pennies. How can that be right?"

The man didn't have anything to say to that. But now I had a question for him.

"What did you eat for breakfast?"

He was so surprised that I'd had the nerve to ask him something, he didn't answer. So I pointed at some of the other MPs, the sympathetic ones. "You then. And you. What did you eat?"

The answers came back:

"Devilled kidneys."

"A kipper."

"Ham and eggs."

I turned to the girls and asked, "And what did you eat, Nell? And you, Mary, Sally, Jen?"

"Nothing."

"Nothing."

"Nothing."

"Nothing."

"Exactly," I said. "And that ain't just because of the strike. That's all most of us get for breakfast every day of the week. Dinnertimes, evenings, we get a slice of bread and a dish of tea, that's all. Sometimes – if we're lucky – we can stretch to a piece of herring. Meat? We see that maybe once in six months. The last time we had any was back in January. Remember that, Nell? God alone knows when we'll have meat again."

I looked around the MPs in that room.

"Gentlemen," I said, "we ain't asking for the moon. We ain't expecting something for nothing. We're hard-working girls. We're on our feet for shifts of twelve hours, sometimes fourteen. How can anyone work that hard and still not have enough to live on? Why do we have to choose between putting food on the table and paying the rent? All we want is fair pay and fair conditions. We don't want to have our wages docked for no reason. We don't want little girls like my sister losing their hair because the boss is too tight-fisted to buy her a trolley to carry the trays on. We don't want to be poisoned when we eat. Just give us a different room to have dinner in!"

Mr whatever-his-name-was hadn't quite given up, and said, "Mr Wilkinson has given me his personal assurance that there's no incidence of phossy jaw in the factory."

I laughed out loud at that. "Well, that's true in a manner of speaking," I said. "But I could take you down the Mile End Road right now and show you maybe one or two hundred girls who used to work for him who've got it. Girls who got sacked when they couldn't hide the fact they were down with the disease. That's why there ain't any phossy jaw in the factory, mister. It's because all those girls have been chucked out and left to rot. Does that strike you as fair? We're talking about people's lives here. Girls. Young women. We just want to live decent, that's all. We want to live to be mothers. Grandmothers. Can you look me in the face and tell me that's unreasonable?"

His silence told me he couldn't.

20

And so it came to pass that in the summer of 1888, questions were asked in the House of Commons about pay and conditions in the match factory. Questions were asked about the health of the girls who worked there. And it was so shaming for Mr George Arthur Wilkinson, who had his eye on a seat in the House of Lords, he agreed to meet us.

We weren't asking for much. And yet the moment the strike committee stepped into that meeting room I could see Mr Wilkinson was brimming with anger. His pride had been wounded by the things people had said about him in the newspapers. His reputation had been damaged and he blamed us for it.

He wanted to smash us down. To trample us into the ground. I could see Mr Wilkinson's thoughts hovering in the air above his head:

Who do they think they are, trying to force me into a corner? A bunch of common girls only fit to wipe my boots on, behaving as if they're my equals. It's scandalous. How has it come to this?

We sat around a table that had been polished so bright I could see my face in it. I ended up right next to Mr Wilkinson and his dog – that horrible big mastiff. I was so close I could feel its heat and see the drool from its great maws pooling on the carpet. And I could also see from the way Mr Wilkinson's jaw was set that he'd refuse all our demands. He was hell-bent on breaking the strike. On breaking every single one of us, no matter how long it took.

And Mr Wilkinson would succeed, because he could afford for this to go on and we couldn't. There was barely anything left in the strike fund and we'd all got thinner and thinner these last two weeks. We'd lose to him, and he would squeeze and squeeze and squeeze until there was no life left in any of us.

The talking started. And it went on. And on. Back and forth, back and forth. Round and round in circles. One hour passed. He wouldn't agree to anything on our list. It was deadlock. Stalemate. Mr Wilkinson wasn't budging an inch.

At the beginning of the second hour of negotiations, I was so tired and frustrated I swore under my breath, "God help us!"

And it was then that something strange happened. The dog that had been at Mr Wilkinson's side got up. It walked to the end of the table and sat down beside Nell. It put its great big head in Nell's lap and whined softly.

And Nell broke into that beautiful, golden, fairy-child smile of hers that lit up her face from inside. The sun came slanting through the window just as Nell laughed out loud. So Mr Wilkinson could see her gums and the holes where her teeth had once been.

Beside me, Mr George Arthur Wilkinson paled a little.

As he looked at Nell – just for a fleeting moment – I knew he didn't see a troublemaker. He saw a twelve-year-old girl who'd had all her teeth pulled from her head by her own father. A twelve-year-old girl who was losing her hair because of the work she did to put money into his pocket. A twelve-year-old girl playing with his dog's ears the way his daughters probably did. The only difference between them was that Nell had the misfortune to be born poor.

"She just wants to be treated fair," I said softly, so only he could hear. "That ain't too much to ask is it, Mr Wilkinson?"

He tore his eyes away from Nell and looked at me properly for the first time. "No," he said very quietly. "No, it isn't."

But Mr Wilkinson was still resisting. Agreeing to our demands was like giving in as far as he was concerned. Worse still, it would mean admitting he'd been in the wrong and his pride couldn't stand that.

Mr Wilkinson looked so uncomfortable that for a moment he reminded me of Father when he came home to Mother after being caught with another woman. Father, standing in the doorway, wondering how he was going to get himself off the hook this time.

But Father never really had to. Because after she'd cried herself out, Mother would find a way of blaming the Other Woman. She'd decide Father had been led astray. He'd had his head turned. He'd been bewitched. Whatever had happened, it was never, ever Father's fault.

It was the only way Mother could keep on holding everything together. If she poured her hate and rage into the Other Woman, she could carry on loving Father. If the Other Woman was to blame, Mother and Father could go on as before.

I looked at Mr Wilkinson, thinking of my parents, and suddenly saw that he needed to be given a way out. A way that gave us what we wanted but that allowed him to keep his pride. He needed to be able to walk out of the meeting room looking and feeling like the important gentleman he thought he was.

Just as I was thinking that, I noticed Mr Fettler hovering in the shadows by the door. And I saw a way of solving everything.

I turned to Mr Wilkinson. I made my face look as blank and as simple as I possibly could. All this time both sides had tried to portray us as innocent, sheep-like girls being exploited by powerful people for their own ends. Well then, why not play that part, just for a bit?

"Can I say something, sir?" I said.

"Yes, of course," Mr Wilkinson replied. But he was looking a bit suspicious, like he thought I was up to something.

I lowered my head as if I was in awe of him. And I said, as if I was truly puzzled and wanted him to explain things to me, "I'm thinking it's a shame how all this happened. It got so out of hand!

But you seem like a fair-minded gentleman, Mr Wilkinson. And a kind one, if I may be so bold. One who'd like to take care of the poor, ignorant girls he's got working for him. I don't understand how a fine, upstanding gentleman such as yourself would risk his workers catching phossy jaw just so he could save himself a few pennies. So I'm wondering if maybe you didn't know about it? Can I ask, sir, does Mr Fettler tell you everything that goes on down on the factory floor? Or does he keep things like that to himself?"

It's an interesting thing, flattery. Say something nice to a girl and they won't believe you. The amount of times I'd told Nell she was beautiful, only for her to go bright pink and bat away the compliment like I was teasing her! But say something flattering to a man, and he puffs himself up and purrs like a cat that's got the cream, even if what you're telling him is a blindingly obvious lie.

I could see the cogs turning in Mr Wilkinson's brain. He was flattered. And I was offering him a way out. A way to make concessions to us and yet retain his reputation. I was handing him someone to blame.

If Mr Wilkinson said he didn't know what had been going on, why then ... he couldn't be accused of being a heartless, shameless exploiter of girls and young women, could he? No ... if he made concessions now, he'd be seen as a generous protector. A good and kind employer, a sort of noble, selfless father figure to his workforce. Mr Wilkinson would look like the respectable owner of a respectable factory and no doubt more people would choose to invest in it.

And so he took the bait I was dangling before him.

"You're quite right," Mr Wilkinson said. He looked at Mr Fettler, assessing him, no doubt weighing up his usefulness, wondering if he was worth hanging on to. Or not.

He suddenly announced to the whole room, "I see now that Mr Fettler hasn't kept me fully informed of problems on the factory floor. And I apologise most sincerely for that. I am very grateful that you have brought these matters to my attention. Please be assured that the situation will be corrected. As for now, your demands shall, of course, be met."

That was it.

We'd won!

We. Had. Won.

There should have been fireworks. Trumpets sounding. A fifty-gun salute.

Instead, there was an astonished pause. I knew the meeting would break up in a moment. I looked at Mr Fettler. He might get the sack, but if he did he'd be replaced by a man cut from the same cloth and we'd be back to square one. There was something else we needed. I spoke fast.

"Can I propose something else too, sir?" I said. "How about the girls elect a representative? Maybe more than one – maybe a whole committee? Girls who can bypass the foreman and report straight to you. We can keep you informed, like. So you'll get to hear about things straight from the horse's mouth, as it were. If anything crops up, we'll come to you, Mr Wilkinson, and you'll give us a fair hearing, won't you? We can nip any trouble in the bud, so things won't never go as far as another walk-out. How does that sound?"

Mr Wilkinson smiled at me kindly, the way a grandfather might smile on his granddaughter when he was giving her a treat. "That sounds perfectly reasonable," he said. "Agreed."

The look Mr Fettler gave me would have shrivelled a slug. It didn't much matter now whether he stayed or whether he got the push.

We had him over a barrel. All I could do was grin back at him.

21

"All right, God," I said as I walked up west the following Saturday afternoon. "Have it your way. You exist. I admit it."

We were back at work by then, me and Nell. The family were home from Kent. Father had work down the docks again and we'd found a new place to rent. Life went on as before. Nothing had changed and yet somehow everything had.

Me and Nell had taken Jimmy to see how Tower Bridge was getting on, but I'd left the two of them there because I had some business of my own to attend to.

"You did good in there, God," I said as I strolled off down the street alone. "You nudged that dog to go sit with Nell, didn't you? And you shone that ray of sunlight through the window. But I did the rest, didn't I? So I believe in you, but you know what? I believe in me too. I believe in all of us. We've got power, haven't we, when we work together like that? And now we've got our foot in the door, we can chip away at Mr George Arthur Wilkinson until he pays us decent wages and we can work shorter shifts.

"We'll form ourselves a trade union," I continued. "*The Union of Women Matchworkers.* How does that sound? Grand, I reckon. We'll make things better, over time. But we'll do it gradual so Mr Wilkinson will hardly notice it's happening. We'll get it done though. Not just for us, neither. What about the dockers, eh? If Father and his mates go on strike, they could bring the whole of London to its knees. Wouldn't that be something?

"There's plenty to do, ain't there? Plenty wrong with the world you made. But that's Man's fault, not yours. Sorry I blamed you for that. Man designed this system, but maybe a woman can put it right, eh? I'll get cracking first thing Monday morning. But you know what? First of all I'm going to buy me some feathers.

"I've got a hat as big as a cartwheel that needs mending."

Author spotlight

Tanya Landman is an award-winning author who has written over 40 books for children and young people. Her work includes picture books, adventure stories and murder mysteries.

Tanya was born and grew up in Kent and as a child she longed to be a monkey! She was interested in all kinds of wildlife and liked to rescue worms and mend snails' shells with sticky tape. Before she started writing, Tanya had a number of different jobs – in a bookshop, a zoo and as an actor and puppeteer. Now she cannot imagine a day without writing. She says, "I love the fact that I'm now allowed to daydream – I was always in trouble for it at school!"

Many of Tanya's books are about specific times in history and their characters have experiences that are based on real events. For example, in 2015 Tanya won the Carnegie Medal for her novel *Buffalo Soldier* set in America in the aftermath of the Civil War. *Hell and High Water* is inspired by the true story of Thomas Benson, an eighteenth-century Devonshire smuggler. As in

Lightning Strike, Tanya is often inspired by stories of vulnerable young people escaping difficult lives.

Tanya now lives in Devon with two sons, two dogs and a cat.

Background to the novel

London's East End in the 1880s

Lightning Strike is set in the summer of 1888 in London's East End. The narrator, Eliza, and her family live in a small house, sharing beds and overhearing the noises of their neighbours.

At that time, the East End of London was heavily populated with working-class people and families, many of them migrants. They lived in small houses near the factories and docks where they worked and earned very little money. Many people lived like Eliza's family – hoping to earn enough each week just to be able to eat. Since the National Health Service was not established until 1948, people had to pay for medical care. Like many children in poor families, three of Eliza's brothers died when they were babies because the family couldn't afford medicine or food.

Still in the London's East End there were also bigger houses where much wealthier people lived, like the man that Eliza calls "the toff".

Match-making factories and the Match Girls' Strike of 1888

Although Eliza is a fictional character, her life is based on fact. In the 1880s, many workers (including young girls like Eliza) were employed by a match-making factory called Bryant and May. They worked long hours and had to eat in the same room where they worked. Workers were fined if they talked, made a mistake or went to the toilet without asking.

As described in the book, many match workers became ill with phossy jaw. Phossy jaw was a bone cancer caused by contact with phosphorus, a poisonous chemical used in match making. The illness often started with loss of hair and yellowing skin. Then toothache and abscesses would develop. Often the teeth had to be pulled out. The disease could lead on to facial disfigurement, brain damage and death.

In 1888, a social campaigner called Annie Besant wrote an article about the terrible conditions in the match-making factories. Most of the workers were teenage girls. Exactly as in the novel, the managers of the factories initially tried to make their workers sign a letter to say the article was untrue. This failed, and when one of the girls was sacked, the Match Girls' Strike began, with around 1,400 workers stopping work.

This was brave. Just like Eliza and Nell in the book, most of the workers had no other income and relied on support from public donations. For about three weeks, the campaigners marched through the London streets and held public meetings. Eventually, the factory owners agreed to stop fining the workers. At the end of July 1888, the Union of Women Match Makers held their first meeting.

Education

The novel is set in the Victorian era, when the importance of education was starting to be recognised. Some schools did exist and in 1880 the Education Act made going to school compulsory, but only for children up to the age of ten.

Fourteen-year-old Eliza and her younger sister Nell, like many other children, worked in the factory instead of going to school. It is implied in "words were dancing on the page" that Eliza has dyslexia and struggles with reading and writing, but a diagnosis or support would not have been available to her. The priority would have been earning money for her family.

Women's rights

At the time the novel is set, some middle-class women were beginning to have rights of their own. For example, in 1868 the University of London started to accept women students. In 1882, the Married Women's Property Act gave wives control over any money they earned. But these rights meant nothing in poorer families where even the children needed to work. It wasn't until 1928 that women were given the same right to vote as men. If Eliza were a real person, being able to vote would be a moment she would enjoy – but it wouldn't happen until she was 64 years old!

Eliza tells us: "Once a girl was sixteen or maybe seventeen she'd get married and start having babies. And then she'd have her hands so full she'd have to stop working at the factory."

Eliza's mother worries her daughter might not get married, but Eliza isn't keen on married life. The women she knows are often beaten by their husbands and have a lot of children to look after. They can't leave because they have no money of their own. It was very unusual for a woman to have a career or live on her own, especially if she was from a poorer background.

Speakers' Corners

"There were always men making speeches in the park. Standing on soapboxes, yelling at anyone who was fool enough to stop and listen."

Eliza is used to seeing people making speeches in the London parks. One place where this still happens is Speakers' Corner in Hyde Park, London. This spot has been used for public meetings and speeches since Victorian times, and even today you will find people there, talking about issues they feel passionate about. The soapboxes that were used for standing on would have been wooden crates used for packing soap. Nowadays, you might hear someone saying "get off your soapbox" or "stop soapboxing".

Socialism

The character Mrs Billingham is a socialist. According to socialism, a person's life chances shouldn't be decided by whether they are born rich or poor, and wealth and power should be fairly shared out. Mrs Billingham's views are in contrast to Eliza's experiences. "People like us didn't get to choose where we ended up," says Eliza. Her family's life chances have definitely been decided by the fact that they were born poor.

Mr George Arthur Wilkinson, who owns the match factory where Eliza works, is not a socialist.

As a business owner, he is rich and he has control over the lives of the people who work for him. He could choose to improve their working conditions and pay them more fairly, but does he?

Religion

"Mother was a devoted Christian. She said everything that happened was God's will. He moved in mysterious ways and we had to accept it with good grace." Eliza's mother is a Victorian church-goer and expects all the children to attend church with her, dressed in their Sunday best. At this time, religion was part of most people's lives, but the nineteenth century was also the first time in England that public figures like politicians started to be open about having no religious beliefs.

Eliza questions her mother's faith. She says, "How was I supposed to thank God for making us poor and hungry and desperate?"

Statue of the Prime Minister

In the novel, a statue of William Gladstone, the Prime Minister between 1868 and 1894, stands near the gates of the match factory. This is a real statue that you can see today if you visit this corner of London. Gladstone was a hero to Bryant and May, who owned the match factory that was on this site, and they erected the statue to honour him.

According to the novel and to some historic accounts, the statue was paid for by the money deducted from the match workers' earnings. Even now, the statue's hands are always painted red and are a reminder of the unfairness of overworked and underfed children paying for a wealthy business owner to honour his hero. If anyone tries to clean the hands, someone paints them red again overnight!

Activism and campaigners

This novel is dedicated to "campaigners everywhere" and begins with a quote from Greta Thunberg, a famous young activist who has united people about an important cause. Since 2018, Thunberg has led a global environmental campaign to get world leaders to do something about climate change before it is too late.

Lightning Strike describes public meetings, speeches and marches. All this creates a lot of publicity. Eliza says, "Being one of a crowd makes you feel bigger. Better. I was one small person, and yet I could feel a power within me that week that grew and grew until I felt like I could defeat dragons." An important part of Eliza's story is how she learns that by uniting with others, she can make a difference.

Who's who in this novel

Eliza is the main character and tells the story. Like many of her friends, Eliza is employed at a match-making factory. But she is also different – she is angry about the way her family has to live and she isn't interested in marriage and children.

Nell is Eliza's younger sister, who also works in the match-making factory.

Eliza's mother is a woman of strong Christian beliefs. She knows that her husband has affairs with other women but always forgives him. She wants Eliza to grow up to have the security of a husband too.

Eliza's father works at the dockyard in London's East End. He is not a faithful husband, but he is a better father than most of the others in the neighbourhood.

Jimmy is Eliza's younger brother, who is fascinated by bridge building and hates being clean enough to go to church on Sundays.

Mr and Mrs Jones are neighbours of Eliza and her family. At the beginning of the story, Mrs Jones is very ill with phossy jaw.

Mary Delaney, Long Tall Sally and Little Jen are Eliza's friends, who keep her company at the music hall. They are part of the group that talk to Mrs Billingham about conditions at the factory.

Ma Lambert is an older woman who works at the match-making factory. She remembers when the statue of the Prime Minister was unveiled and gets involved in the fight about conditions at the factory.

Mr George Arthur Wilkinson owns the match-making factory, carries a silver-topped cane and has a fierce dog.

Mr Fettler, the foreman at the match-making factory, is cruel and harsh, and has a lot of power over the workers.

Mrs Millicent Billingham is a socialist activist who impresses Eliza with a speech about equal rights.

What to read next

After the War by Tom Palmer

In the summer of 1945, three hundred children rescued from Nazi concentration camps arrive in the English countryside. But after such horror, what will it take for them to recover? An easy-to-read, touching and important story about friendship and hope.

Buffalo Soldier by Tanya Landman

The story of Charley, a "freed" slave who pretends to be a boy and joins the army. The author's research brings the book to life. Racism, war and identity are all important themes. An exciting yet brutal story set in the 1860s in America.

Here I Stand: Stories that Speak for Freedom by Amnesty International

A collection of stories, graphic narratives and poetry by twenty-five writers, including Neil Gaiman, Sarah Crossan and Francis Hardinge. These are shocking and eye-opening stories that will make readers think about the importance of standing up for human rights.

The Girl with No Nose by Georgia Byng

"Pancake Face" Alice Peasbody was born with no nose, and her life in Victorian England is full of cruelty. How will she cope when she moves to the city? This is a book about difference and kindness, and it was inspired by a Victorian false nose at the Hunterian Museum in London.

What do you think?

1. Eliza hasn't had a proper education. How might her life have been different if she'd had proper schooling?

2. In the time the novel is set, women's rights are very limited. If you were Eliza and Nell, what would be the top three changes you'd make to women's and girls' lives?

3. At one point, a "toff" looks at Eliza and Nell as if they are worthless. What, if anything, makes one person better than another?

4. Have you ever wanted something as much as Eliza wants her new hat? What made it so desirable? Did you get it by asking or saving up? Or are you still waiting?

5. Eliza's mother says, "God works in mysterious ways." How has Eliza's attitude to God changed by the end of the novel?

6. Mrs Billingham takes the view that people should fight for equality, but Eliza's mother says Eliza must accept the life she has. Who do you agree with, and why?

7. Eliza and her friends campaign for their rights. Is there a cause that you want to fight for? Even if you can't go on a march, what social action could you take? For example, could you write to your MP or volunteer to help a local group?

8. What do you think about the last line of the book? What does it suggest about Eliza's future?

Word list

bewitching: so beautiful or interesting that you cannot think about anything else

cesspit: hole in the ground for waste

codswallop: nonsense or rubbish

dividends: profits paid to people who own shares in a company

divine intervention: miracle or act of god

docker: someone who works moving goods on and off ships

dwindling: getting smaller

exploiter: someone who treats others unfairly

famine: lack of food over a long period of time

feckless: irresponsible

foreman: man in charge of other workers

hapless: unlucky

heckling: interrupting by shouting out

leprosy: an infectious, painful illness that causes damage to people's flesh

makeshift: temporary and often poor quality

maws: mouth and jaws

phosphorus: poisonous chemical used to make matches

phossy jaw: a bone cancer caused by contact with phosphorus

plinth: platform

Quaker: a member of a Christian group

rally: large public meeting

shareholders: people who own shares in a company

soapboxes: crates or small platforms to stand on to make a speech

socialist: person who believes in socialism – equality between the rich and the poor

solidarity: support because of shared feelings

threadbare: thin and worn

tight-fisted: not willing to spend much money

toff: disapproving slang word for a rich person

urchin: a poor, dirty child

Super-Readable
ROLLERCOASTERS

Super-Readable Rollercoasters are an exciting new collection brought to you through a collaboration between Oxford University Press and specialist publisher Barrington Stoke. Written by bestselling and award-winning authors, these titles are intended to engage and enthuse, with themes and issues matched to the readers' age.

The books have been expertly edited to remove any barriers to comprehension and then carefully laid out in Barrington Stoke's dyslexia-friendly font to make them as accessible as possible. Their shorter length allows readers to build confidence and reading stamina while engaging in a gripping, well-told story that will ensure an enjoyable reading experience.

**Other titles available in the
Super-Readable Rollercoasters series:**

Edgar & Adolf by Phil Earle and Michael Wagg

Rat by Patrice Lawrence

I am the Minotaur by Anthony McGowan

Out of the Rubble by Sally Nicholls

Dark Peak by Marcus Sedgwick

Free online teaching resources accompany all the titles in the Super-Readable Rollercoasters series and are available from:

http://www.oxfordsecondary.com/superreadable